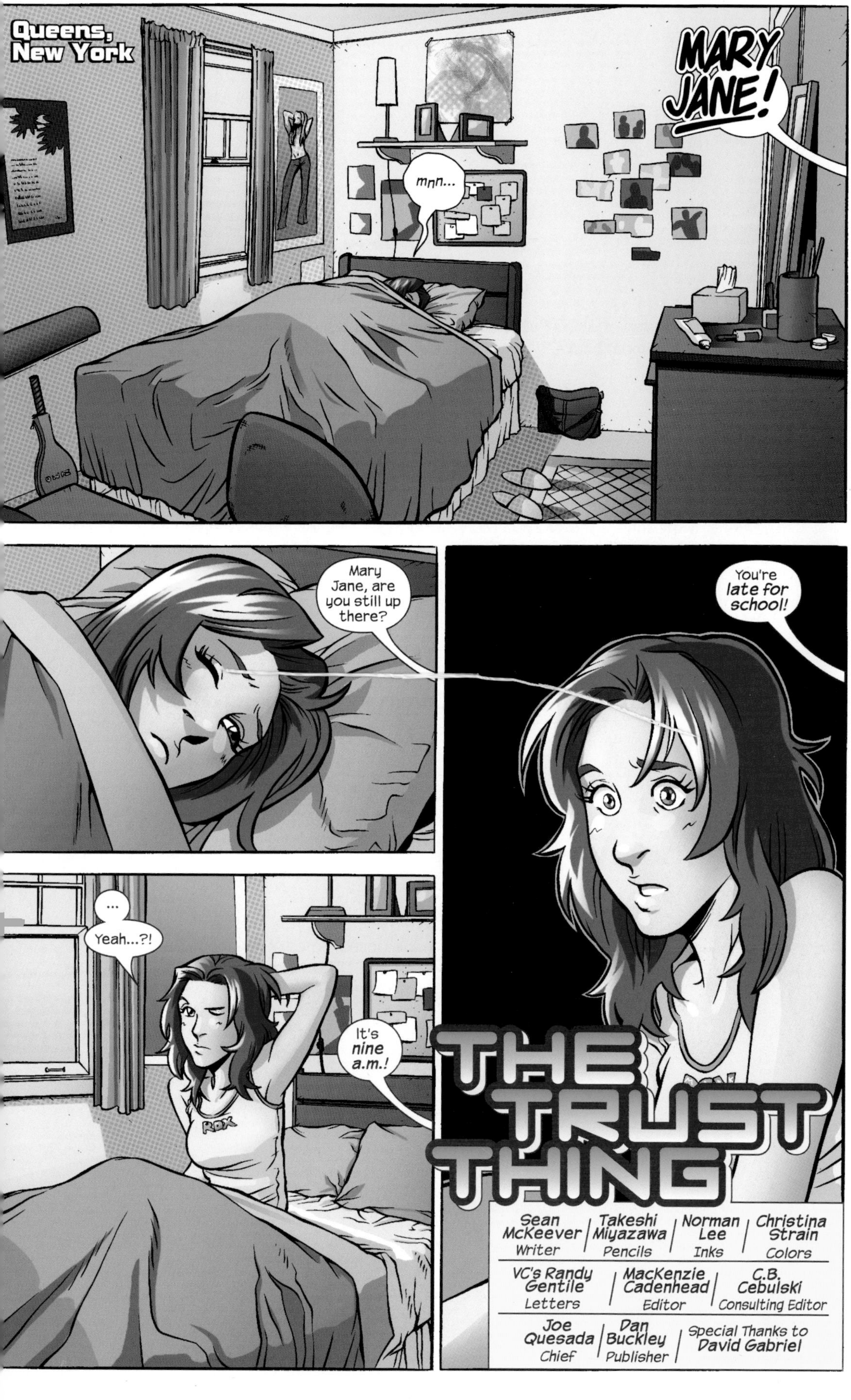
Queens, New York
MARY JANE!
mnn...
Mary Jane, are you still up there?
You're late for school!
...
Yeah...?!
It's nine a.m.!
THE TRUST THING
Sean McKeever Writer
Takeshi Miyazawa Pencils
Norman Lee Inks
Christina Strain Colors
VC's Randy Gentile Letters
MacKenzie Cadenhead Editor
C.B. Cebulski Consulting Editor
Joe Quesada Chief
Dan Buckley Publisher
Special Thanks to David Gabriel

VISIT US AT
www.abdopub.com

Spotlight, a division of ABDO Publishing Company Inc., is the school and library distributor of the Marvel Entertainment books.

Library bound edition © 2006

Library of Congress Cataloging-in-Publication Data

The Trust Thing

ISBN 1-59961-040-X   (Reinforced Library Bound Edition)

All Spotlight books are reinforced library binding and manufactured in the United States of America

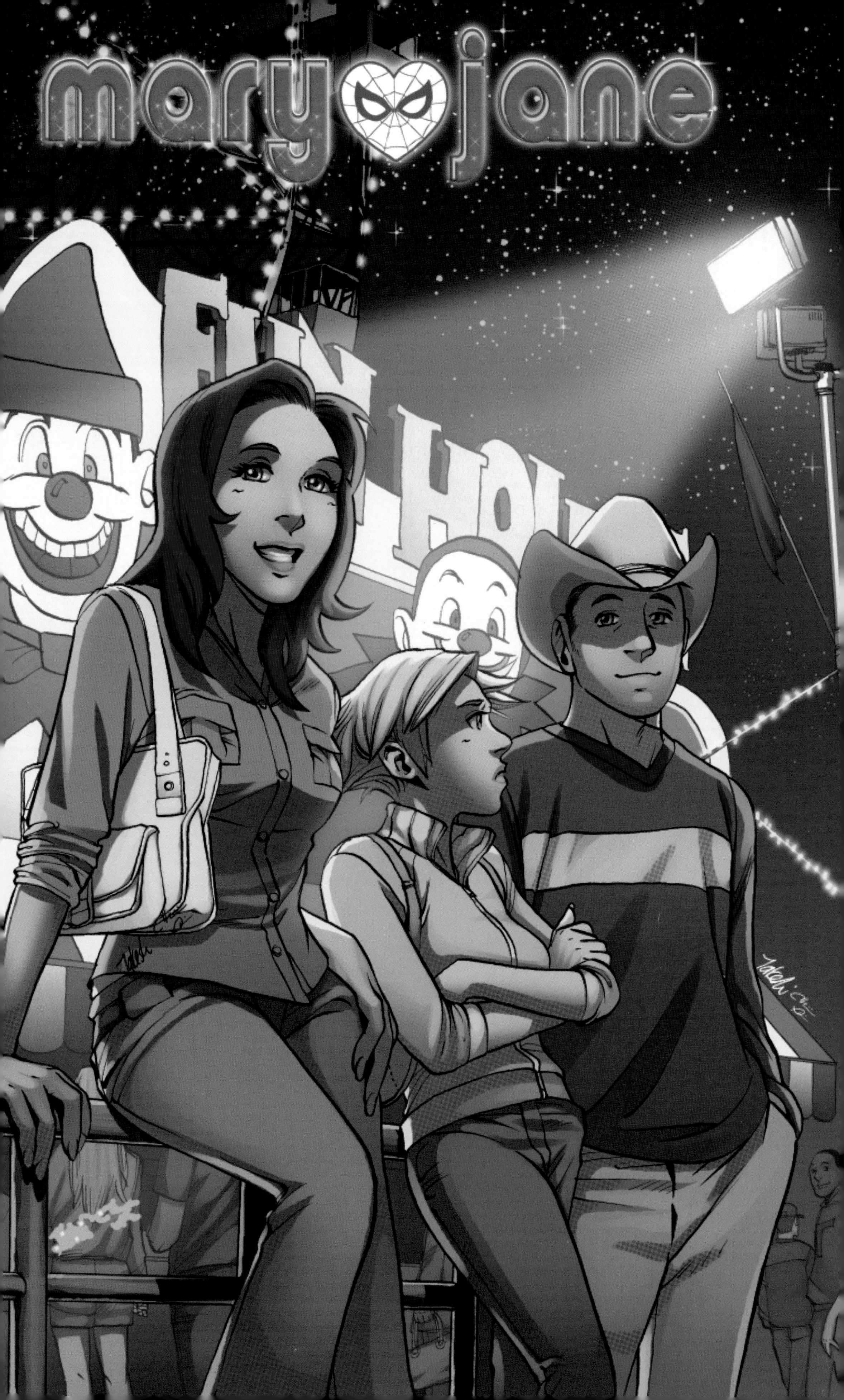
mary jane

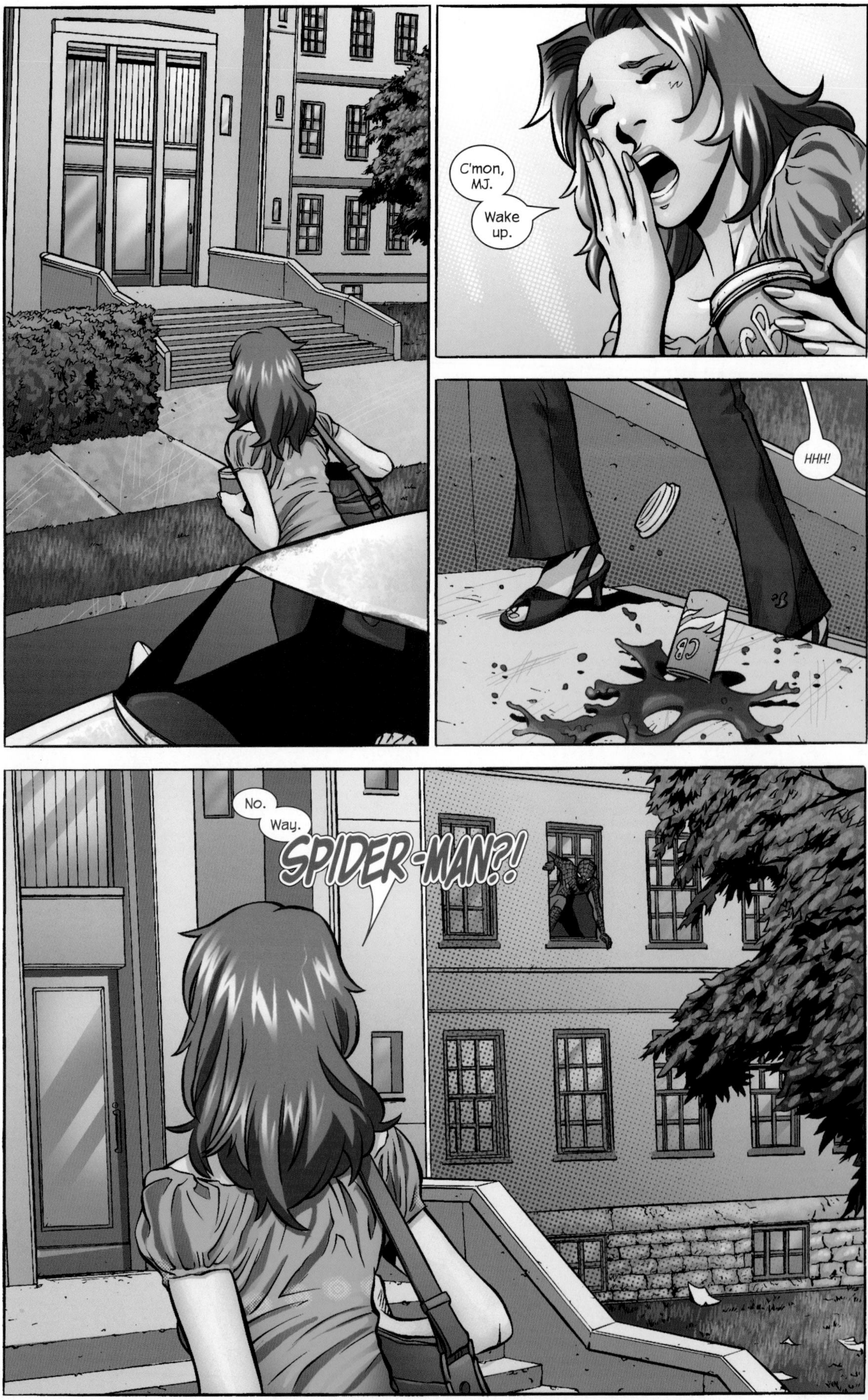
C'mon, MJ.
Wake up.
HHH!
No.
Way.
SPIDER-MAN?!

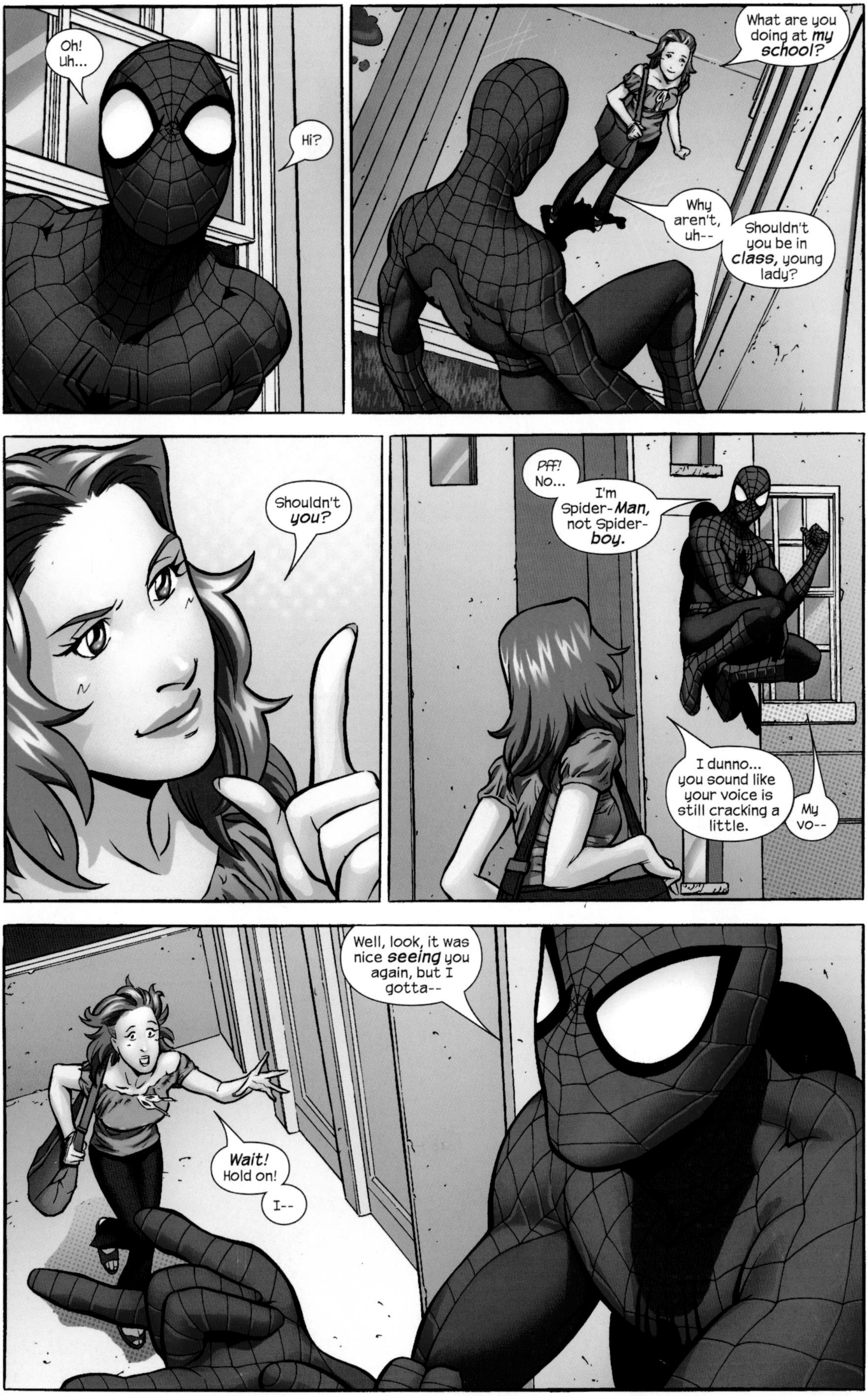

Oh! Uh...
Hi?
What are you doing at *my school?*
Why aren't, uh--
Shouldn't you be in *class,* young lady?
Shouldn't *you?*
Pff! No...
I'm Spider-*Man,* not Spider-*boy.*
I dunno... you sound like your voice is still cracking a little.
My vo--
Well, look, it was nice *seeing* you again, but I gotta--
Wait! Hold on!
I--

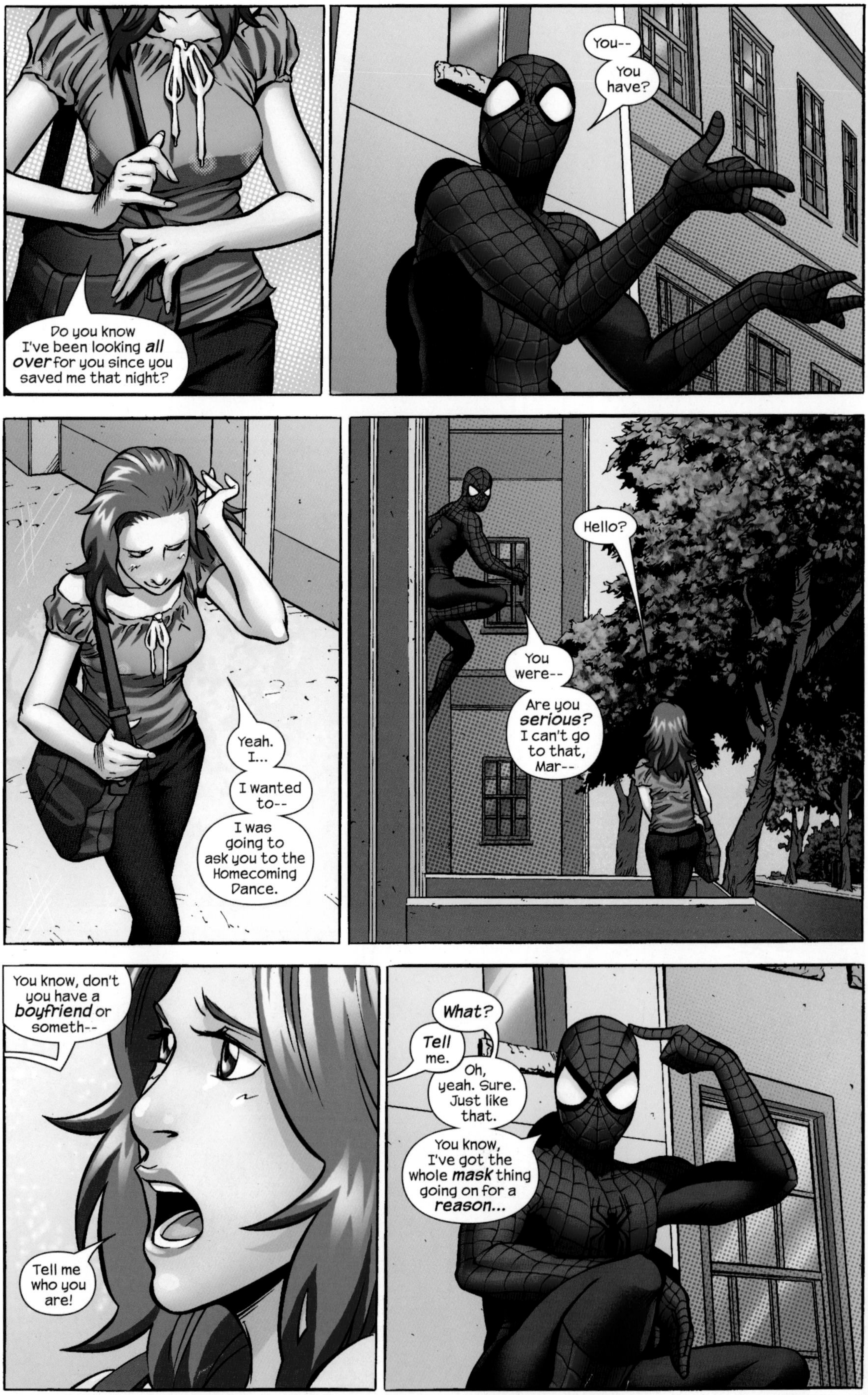
Do you know I've been looking *all over* for you since you saved me that night?
You--
You have?
Yeah. I...
I wanted to--
I was going to ask you to the Homecoming Dance.
Hello?
You were--
Are you *serious?* I can't go to that, Mar--
You know, don't you have a *boyfriend* or someth--
Tell me who you are!
What?
Tell me.
Oh, yeah. Sure. Just like that.
You know, I've got the whole *mask* thing going on for a *reason...*

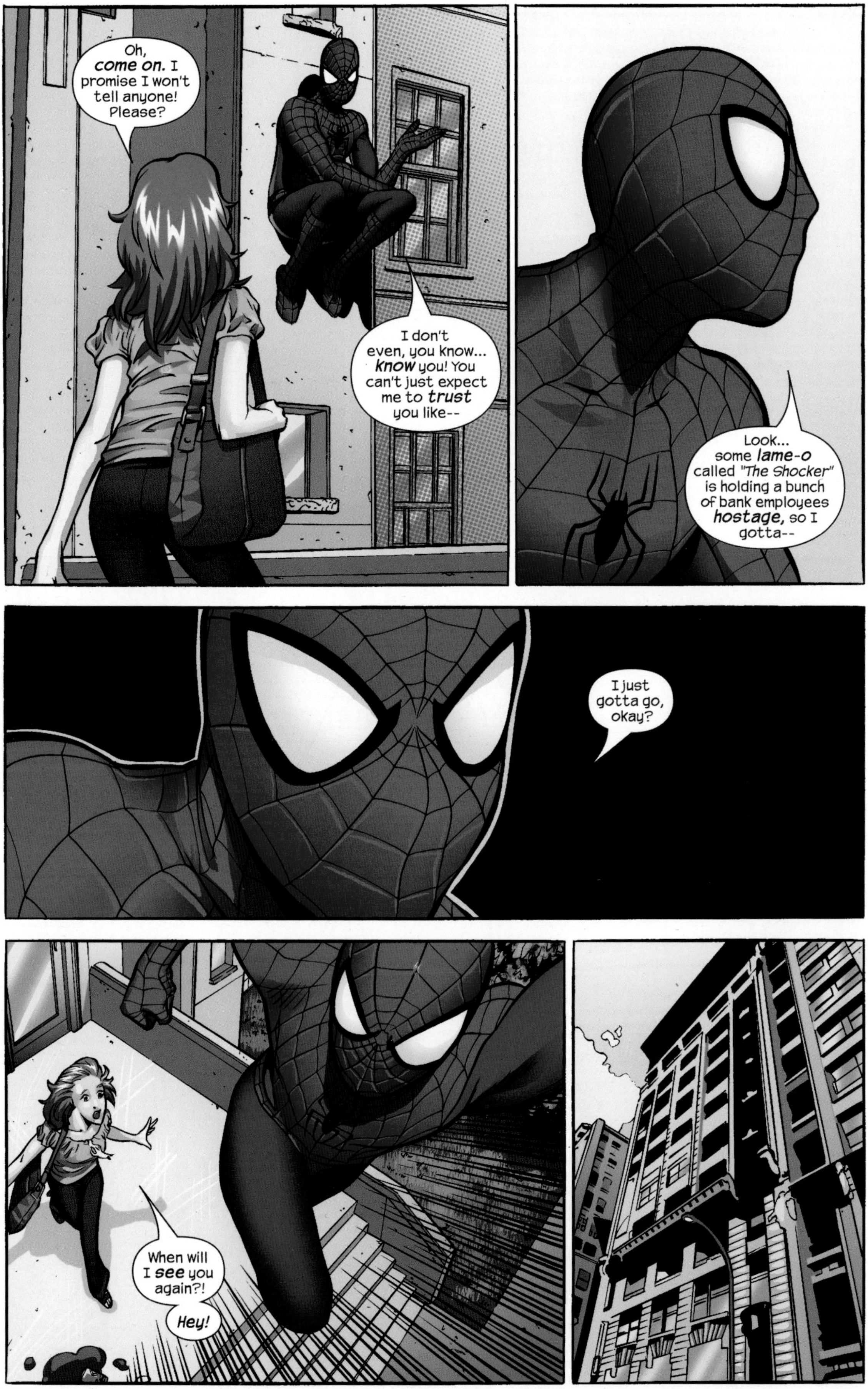

Oh, *come on.* I promise I won't tell anyone! Please?
I don't even, you know... *know* you! You can't just expect me to *trust* you like--
Look... some *lame-o* called *"The Shocker"* is holding a bunch of bank employees *hostage,* so I gotta--
I just gotta go, okay?
When will I *see* you again?!
Hey!

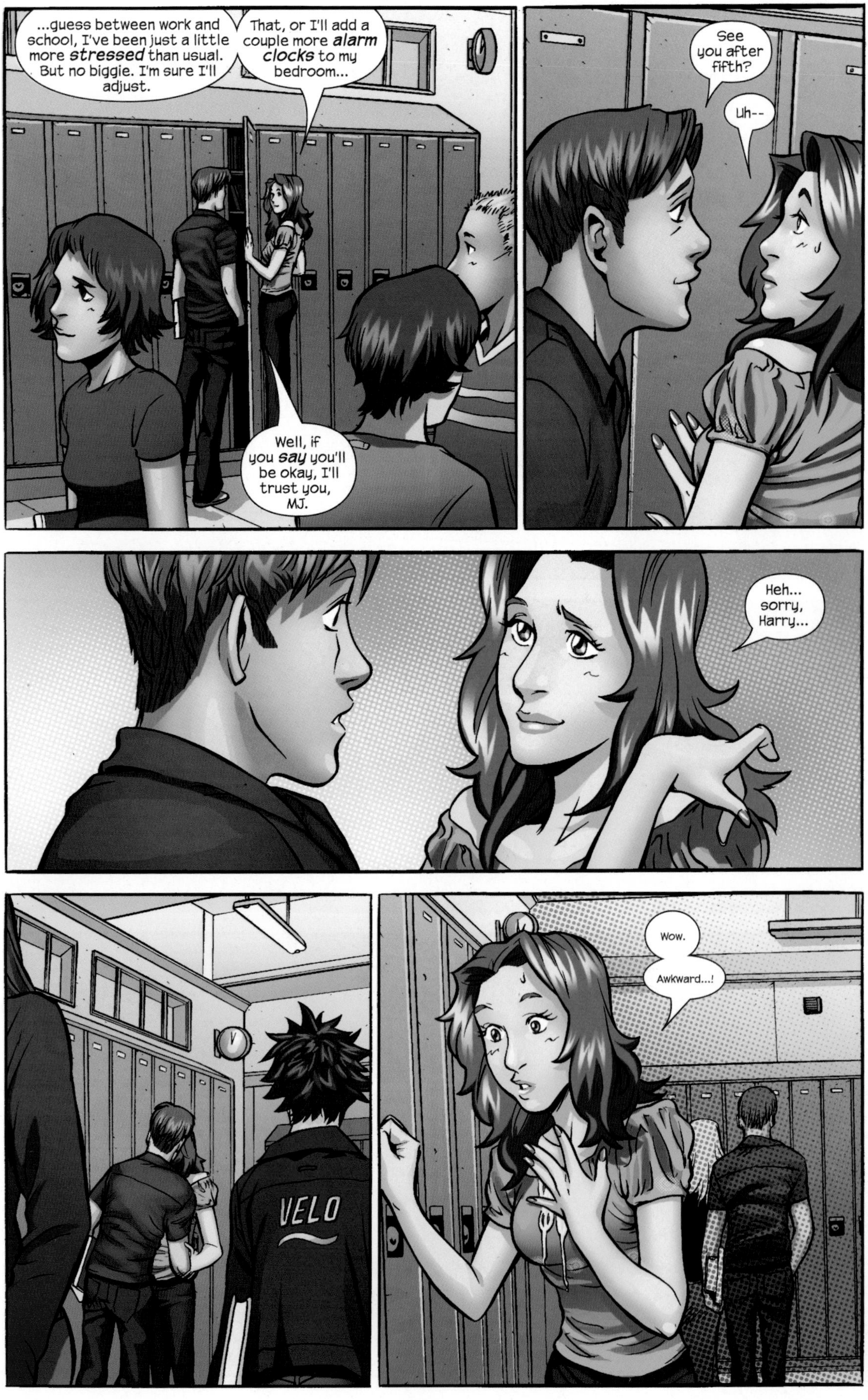

...guess between work and school, I've been just a little more *stressed* than usual. But no biggie. I'm sure I'll adjust.
That, or I'll add a couple more *alarm clocks* to my bedroom...
Well, if you *say* you'll be okay, I'll trust you, MJ.
See you after fifth?
Uh--
Heh... sorry, Harry...
VELO
Wow.
Awkward...!

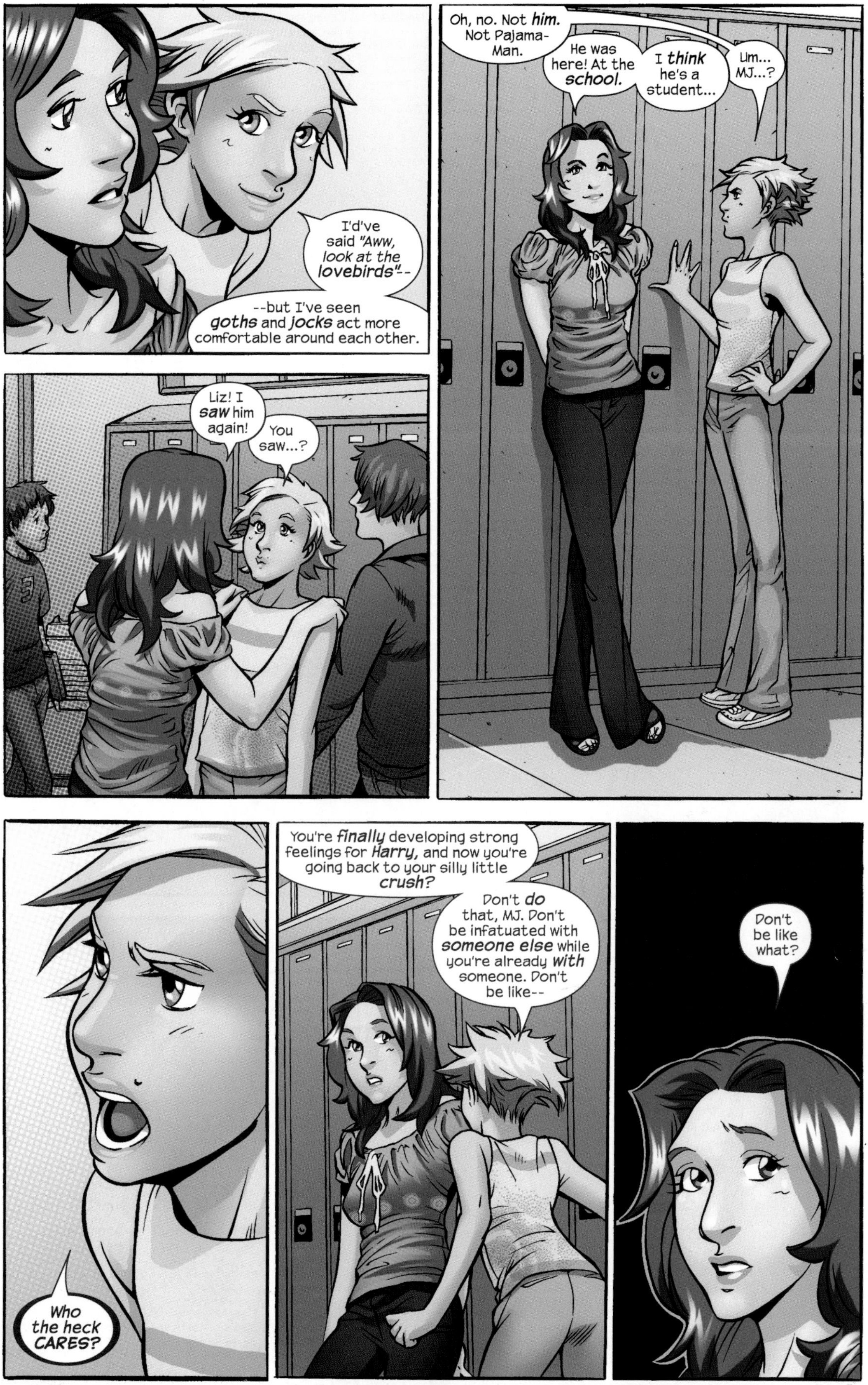

I'd've said "Aww, look at the lovebirds"--
--but I've seen goths and jocks act more comfortable around each other.
Liz! I saw him again!
You saw...?
Oh, no. Not him. Not Pajama-Man.
He was here! At the school.
I think he's a student...
Um... MJ...?
Who the heck CARES?
You're finally developing strong feelings for Harry, and now you're going back to your silly little crush?
Don't do that, MJ. Don't be infatuated with someone else while you're already with someone. Don't be like--
Don't be like what?

Tch. Stupid *Flash.*

He's *cheating* on me, MJ. I know he is.

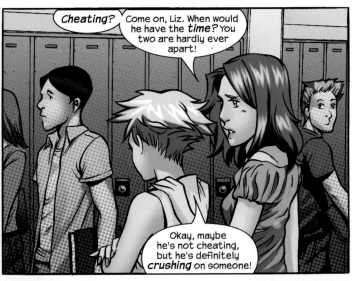

Cheating? Come on, Liz. When would he have the *time?* You two are hardly ever apart!

Okay, maybe he's not cheating, but he's definitely *crushing* on someone!

Uh-- Are-are you *sure?* I mean... how do you know?

Oh, I can just *tell...!* The way he *zones off,* these little *smirks* and *expressions...*

Stupid, dumb jerk.

You have to *help* me!

What?

You're gonna help me find out who that brain donor's *sweet* on. And when we do...

...I'm gonna *kick* her trashy butt to the *moon.*

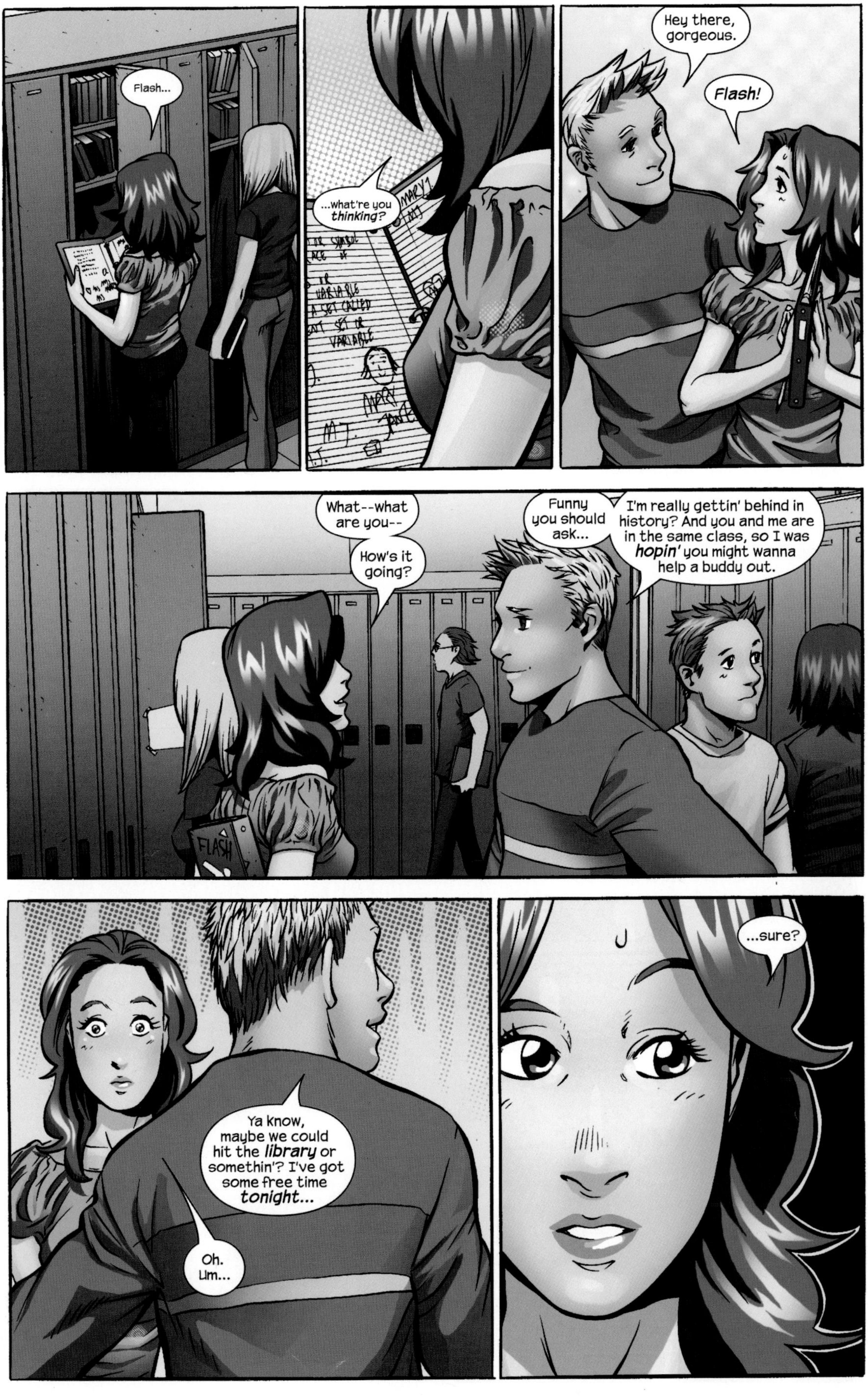
Flash...
...what're you *thinking?*
Hey there, gorgeous.
Flash!
What--what are you--
How's it going?
Funny you should ask...
I'm really gettin' behind in history? And you and me are in the same class, so I was ***hopin'*** you might wanna help a buddy out.
FLASH
Ya know, maybe we could hit the ***library*** or somethin'? I've got some free time ***tonight...***
Oh. Um...
...sure?

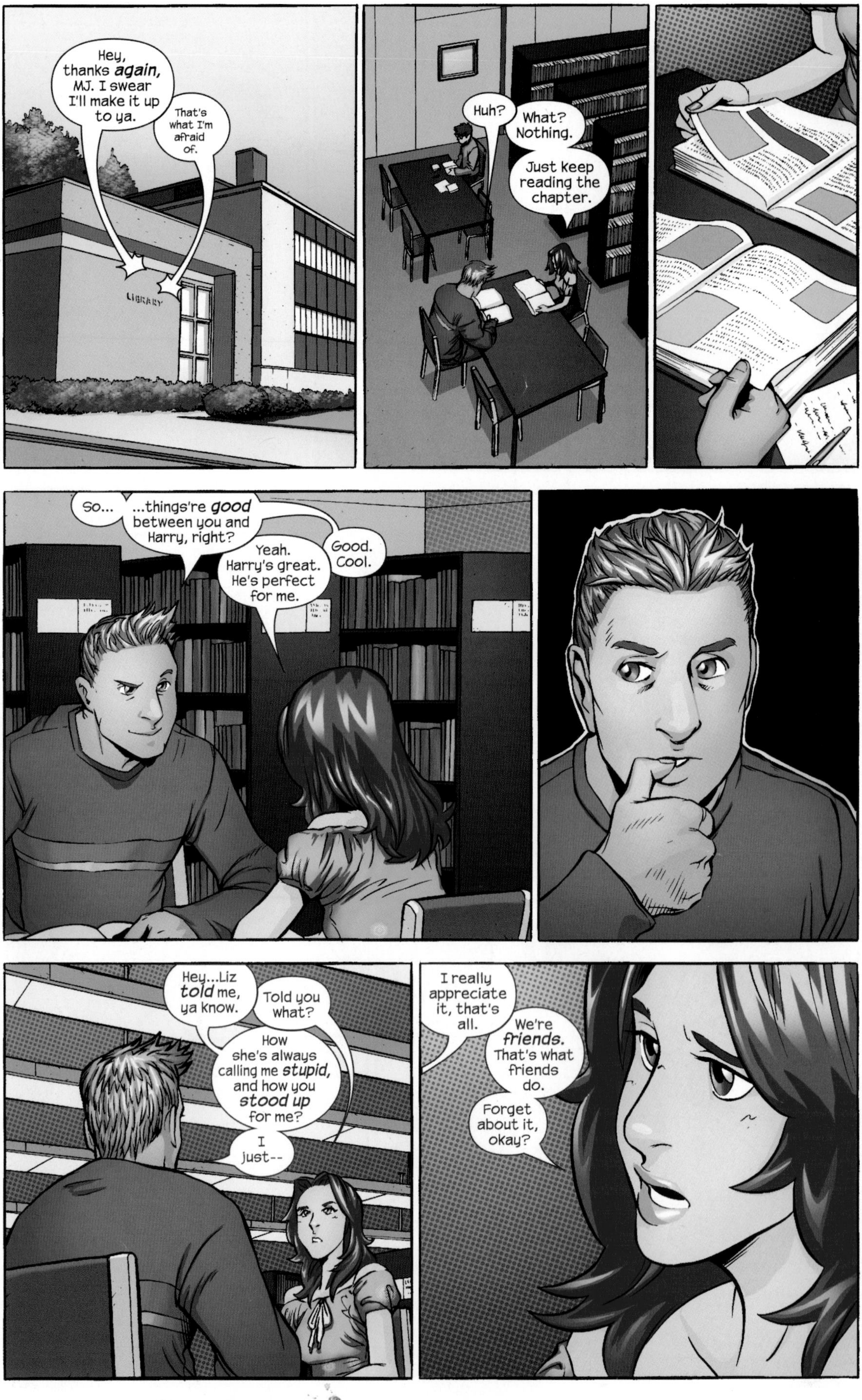
Hey, thanks again, MJ. I swear I'll make it up to ya.
That's what I'm afraid of.
LIBRARY
Huh?
What? Nothing.
Just keep reading the chapter.
So...
...things're good between you and Harry, right?
Yeah. Harry's great. He's perfect for me.
Good. Cool.
Hey...Liz told me, ya know.
Told you what?
How she's always calling me stupid, and how you stood up for me?
I just--
I really appreciate it, that's all.
We're friends. That's what friends do.
Forget about it, okay?

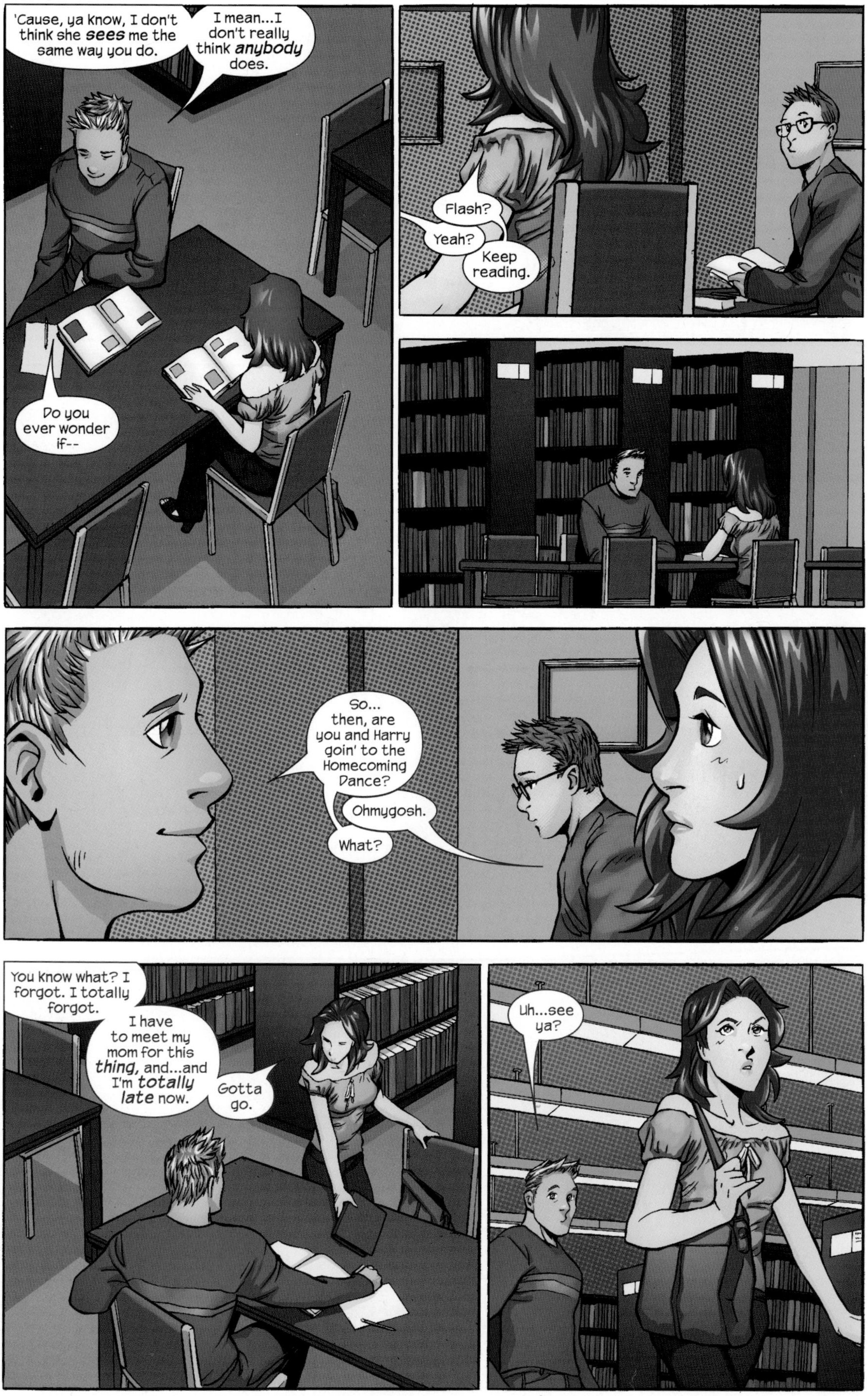
'Cause, ya know, I don't think she sees me the same way you do.
I mean...I don't really think anybody does.
Do you ever wonder if--
Flash?
Yeah?
Keep reading.
So... then, are you and Harry goin' to the Homecoming Dance?
Ohmygosh.
What?
You know what? I forgot. I totally forgot.
I have to meet my mom for this thing, and...and I'm totally late now.
Gotta go.
Uh...see ya?

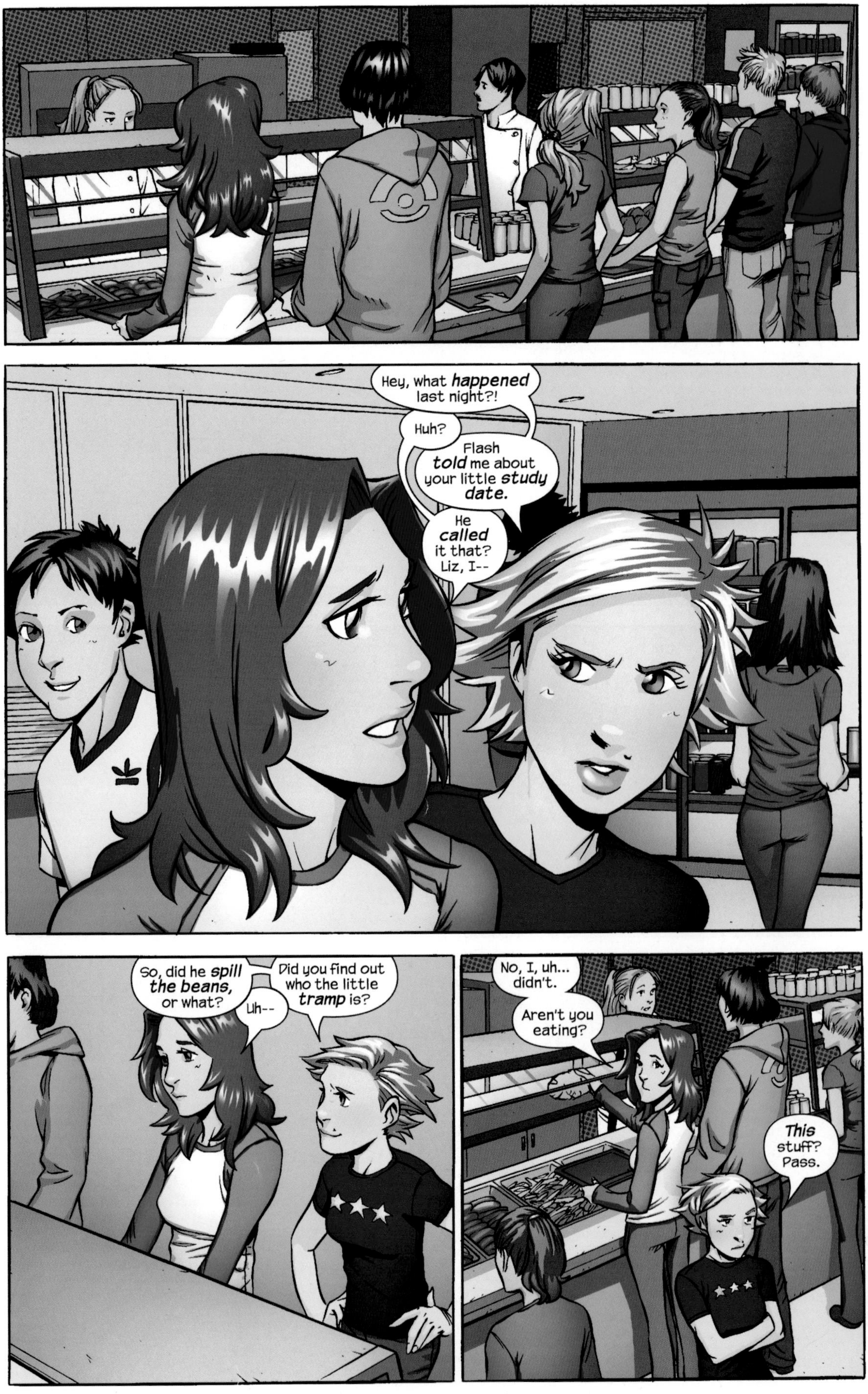
Hey, what happened last night?!
Huh?
Flash told me about your little study date.
He called it that? Liz, I--
So, did he spill the beans, or what?
Uh--
Did you find out who the little tramp is?
No, I, uh... didn't.
Aren't you eating?
This stuff? Pass.

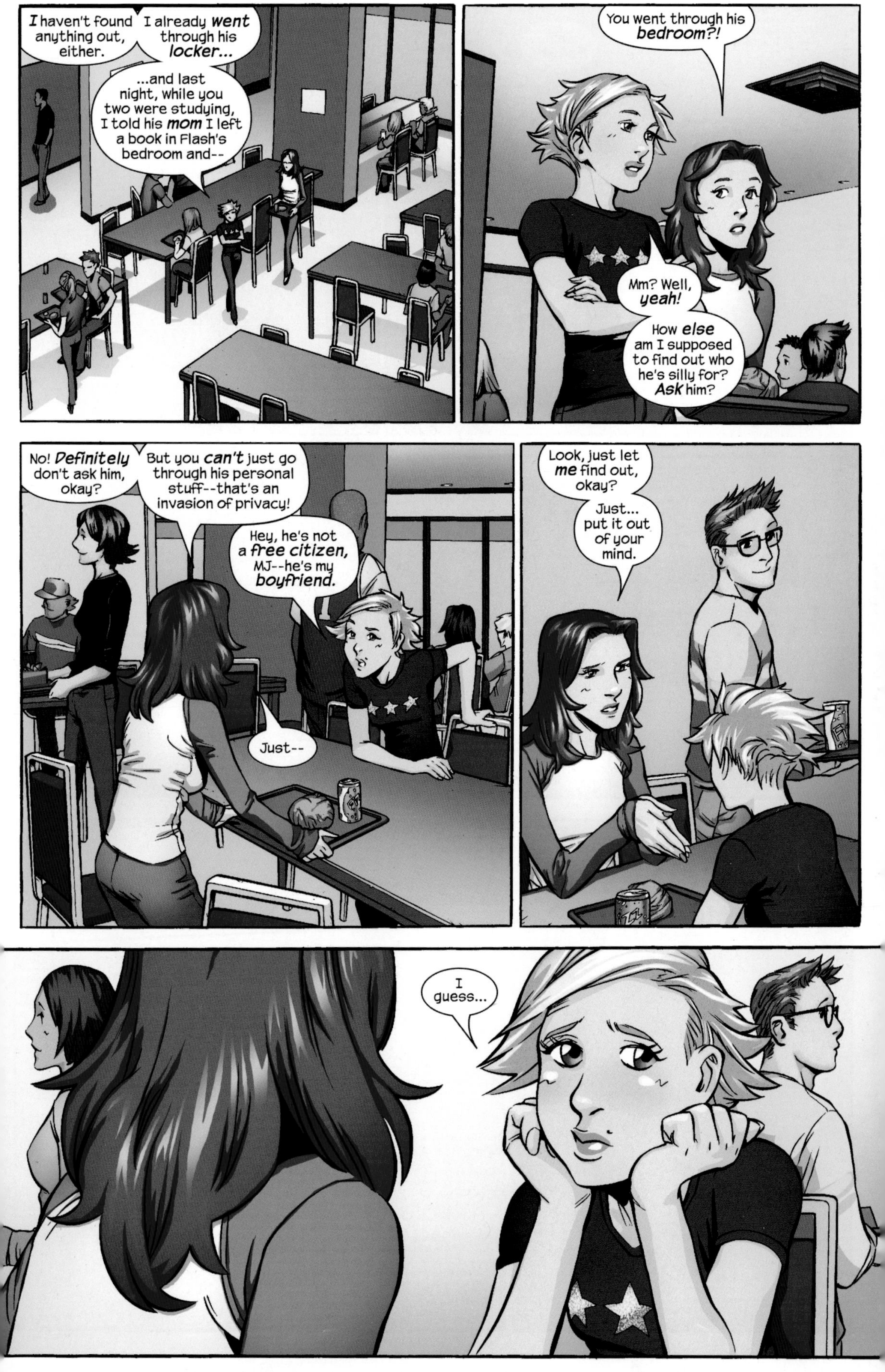

I haven't found anything out, either.
I already went through his locker...
...and last night, while you two were studying, I told his mom I left a book in Flash's bedroom and--
You went through his bedroom?!
Mm? Well, yeah!
How else am I supposed to find out who he's silly for? Ask him?
No! Definitely don't ask him, okay?
But you can't just go through his personal stuff--that's an invasion of privacy!
Hey, he's not a free citizen, MJ--he's my boyfriend.
Just--
Look, just let me find out, okay?
Just... put it out of your mind.
I guess...

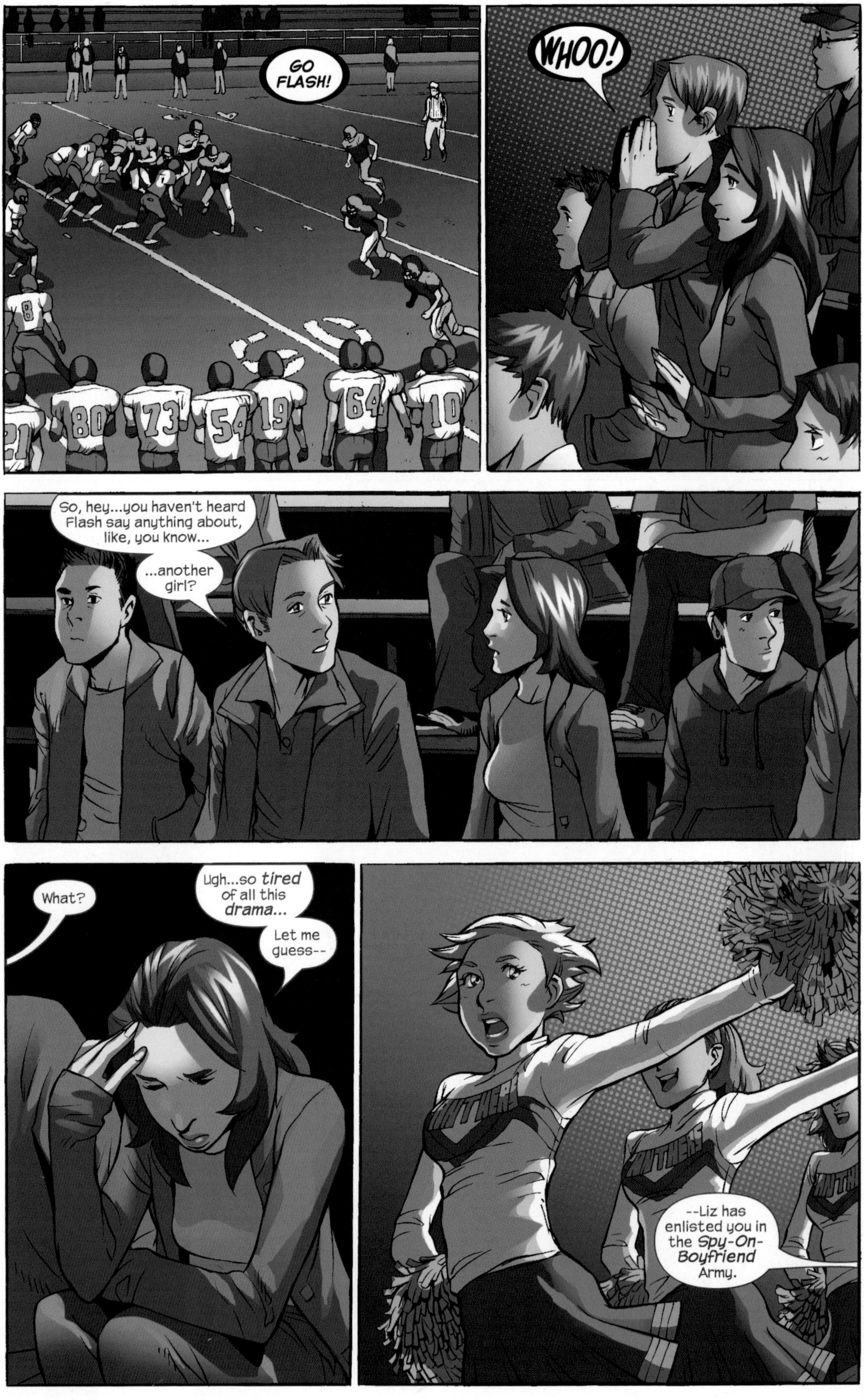
GO FLASH!
WHOO!
So, hey...you haven't heard Flash say anything about, like, you know...
...another girl?
What?
Ugh...so *tired* of all this *drama...*
Let me guess--
--Liz has enlisted you in the *Spy-On-Boyfriend* Army.

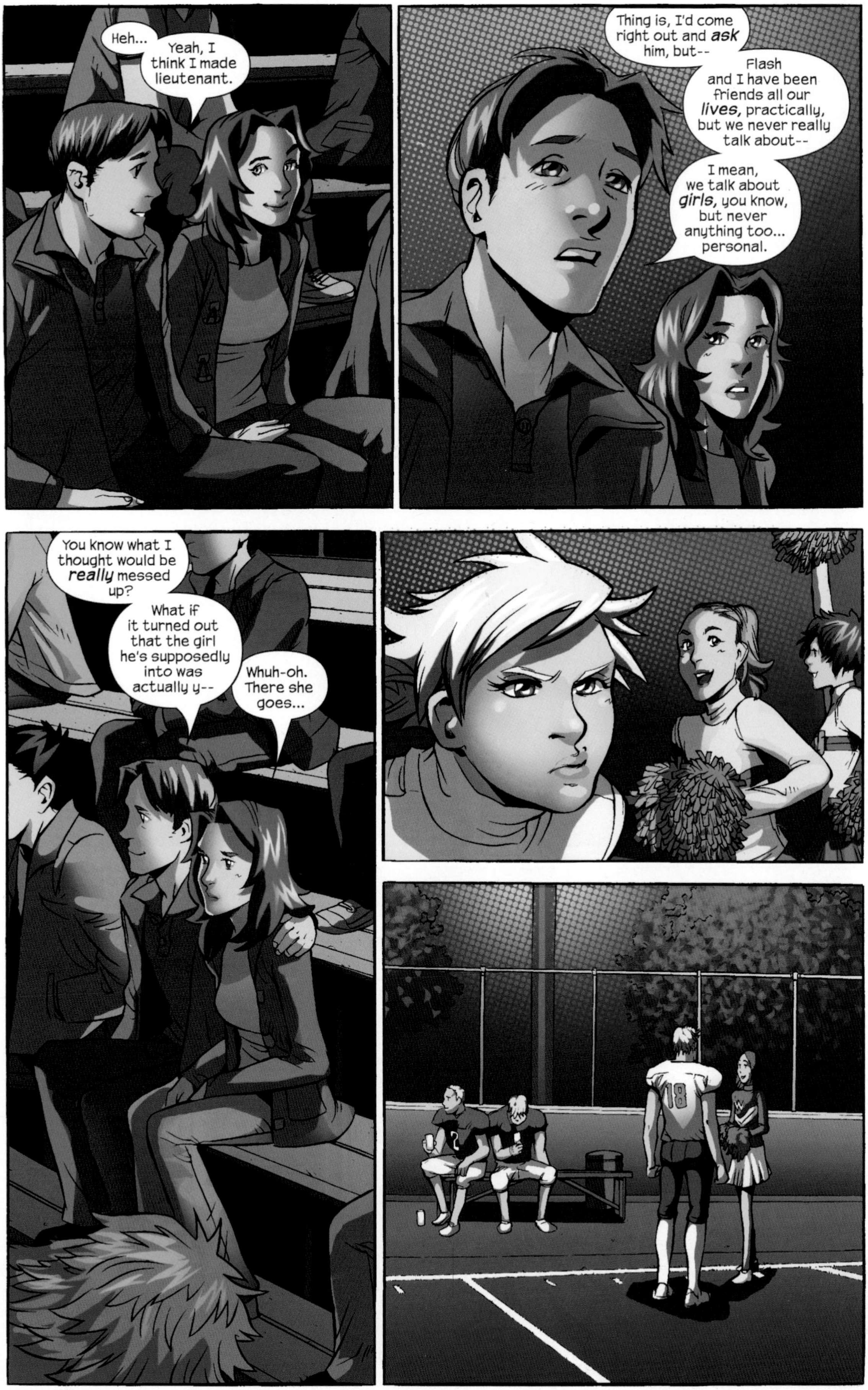
Heh...
Yeah, I think I made lieutenant.
Thing is, I'd come right out and **ask** him, but--
Flash and I have been friends all our ***lives,*** practically, but we never really talk about--
I mean, we talk about ***girls,*** you know, but never anything too... personal.
You know what I thought would be ***really*** messed up?
What if it turned out that the girl he's supposedly into was actually y--
Whuh-oh. There she goes...

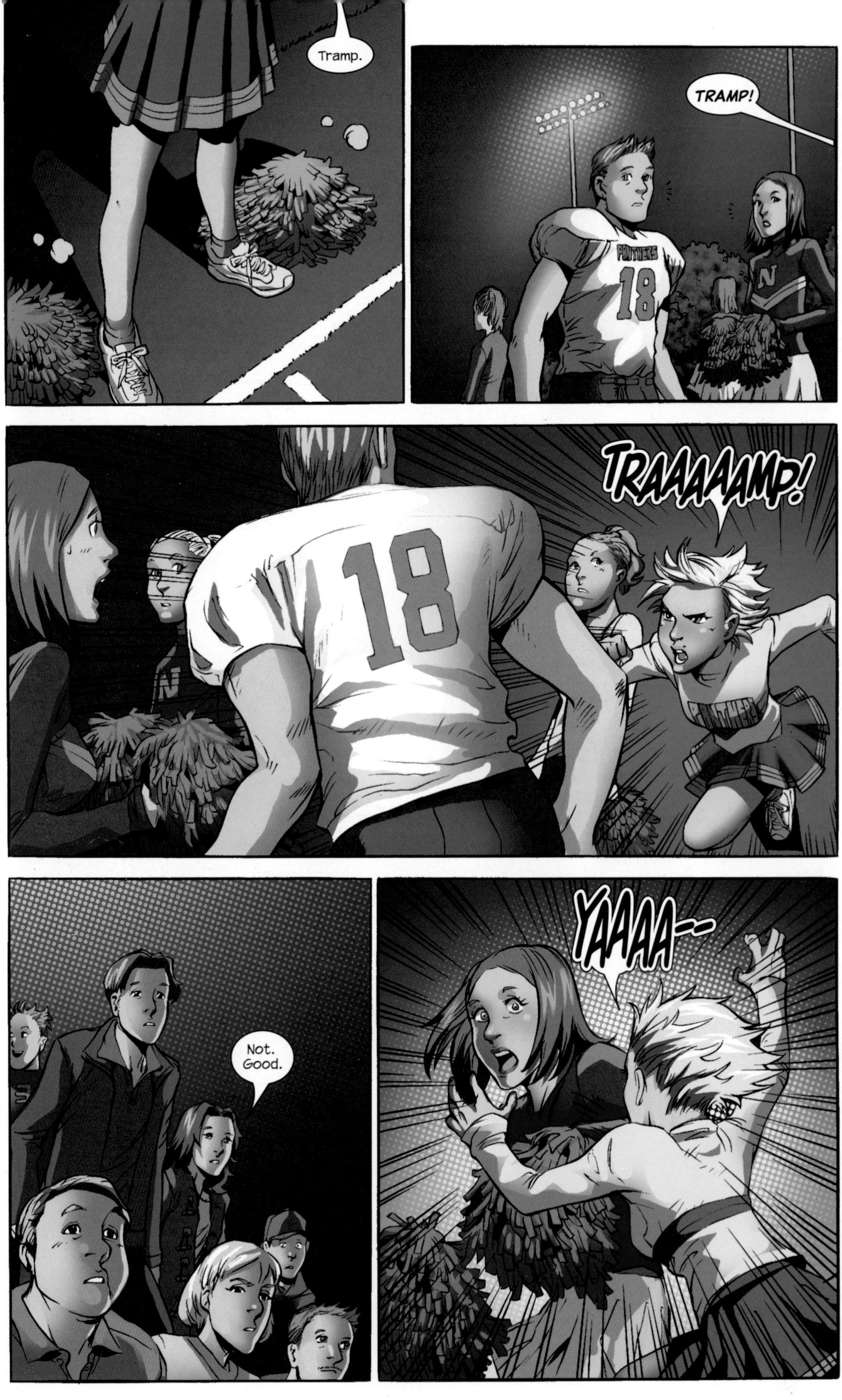
Tramp.
TRAMP!
TRAAAAAMP!
Not.
Good.
YAAAA--

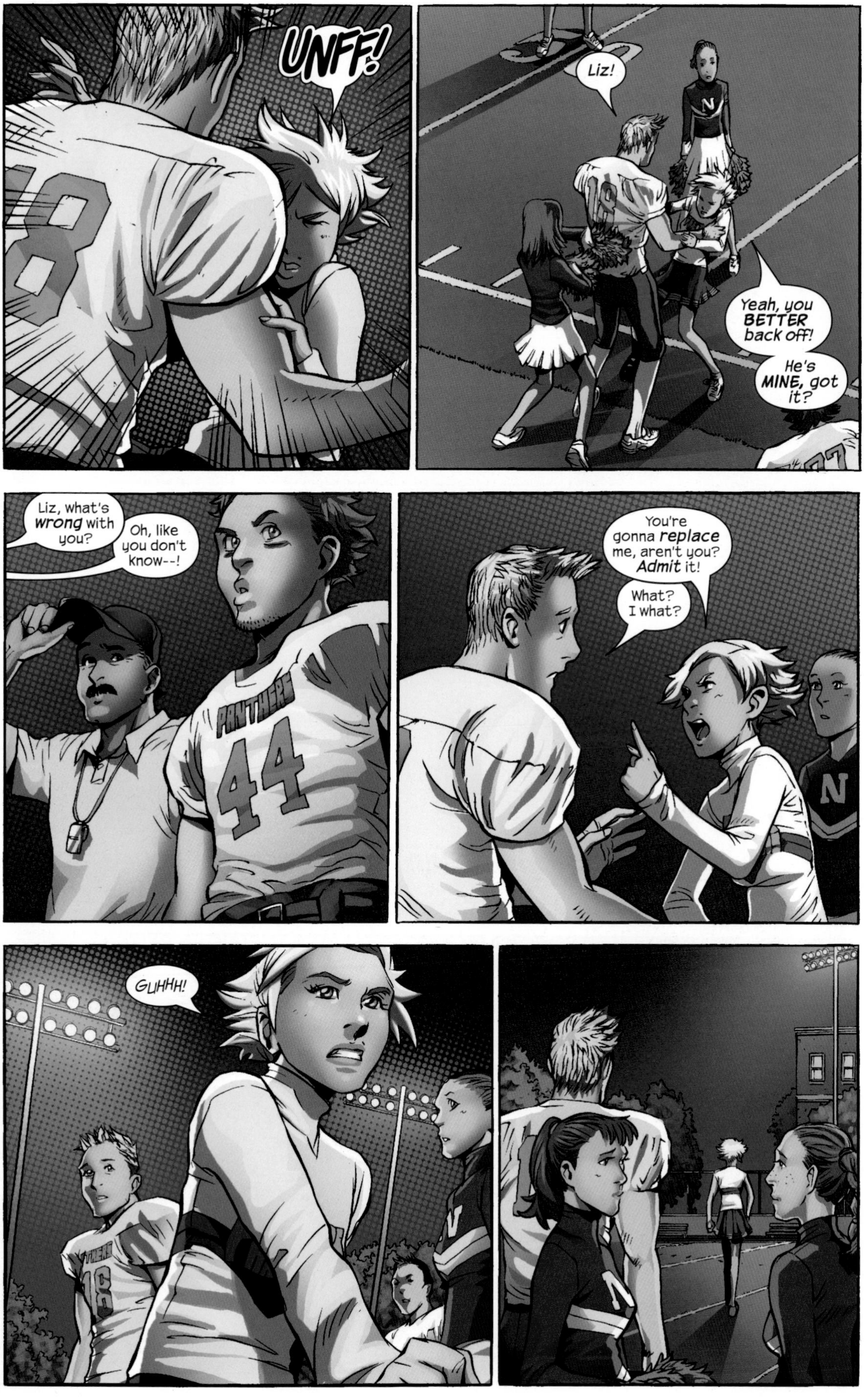
UNFF!
Liz!
Yeah, you BETTER back off!
He's MINE, got it?
Liz, what's wrong with you?
Oh, like you don't know--!
PANTHERS
44
You're gonna replace me, aren't you? Admit it!
What? I what?
GUHHH!

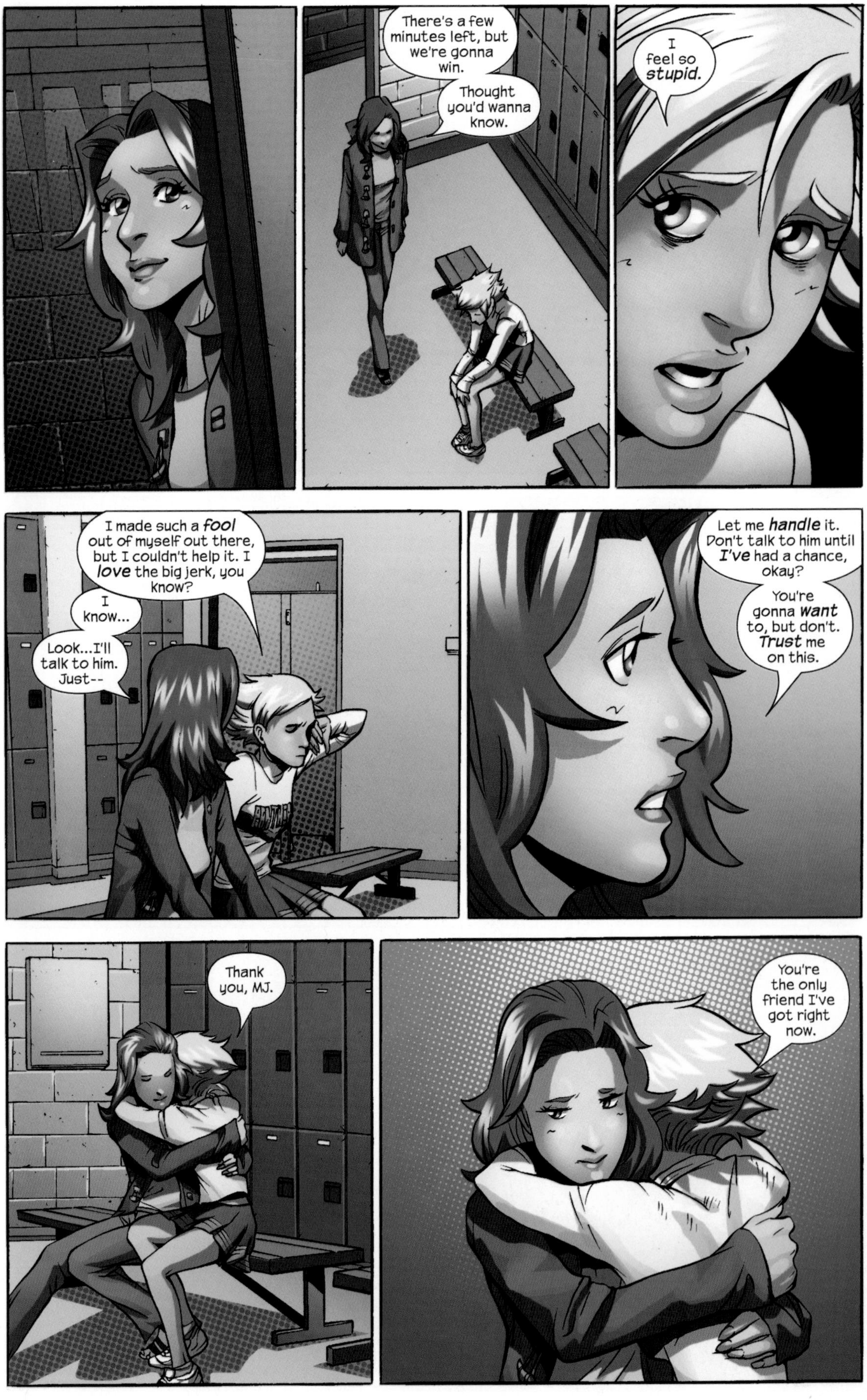
There's a few minutes left, but we're gonna win.
Thought you'd wanna know.
I feel so *stupid.*
I made such a *fool* out of myself out there, but I couldn't help it. I *love* the big jerk, you know?
I know...
Look...I'll talk to him. Just--
Let me *handle* it. Don't talk to him until *I've* had a chance, okay?
You're gonna *want* to, but don't. *Trust* me on this.
Thank you, MJ.
You're the only friend I've got right now.

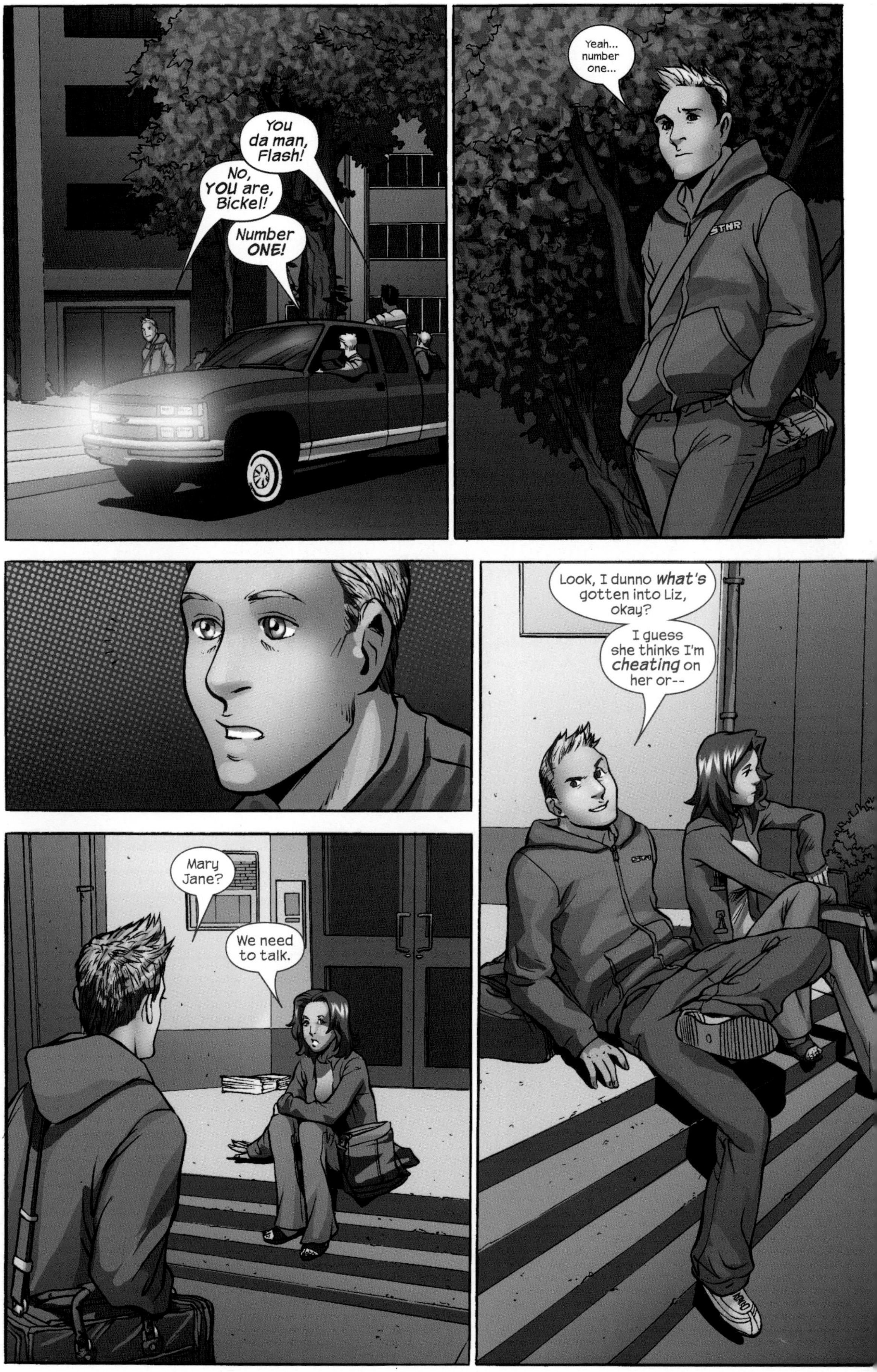
You da man, Flash!
No, YOU are, Bickel!
Number ONE!
Yeah... number one...
Mary Jane?
We need to talk.
Look, I dunno what's gotten into Liz, okay?
I guess she thinks I'm cheating on her or--

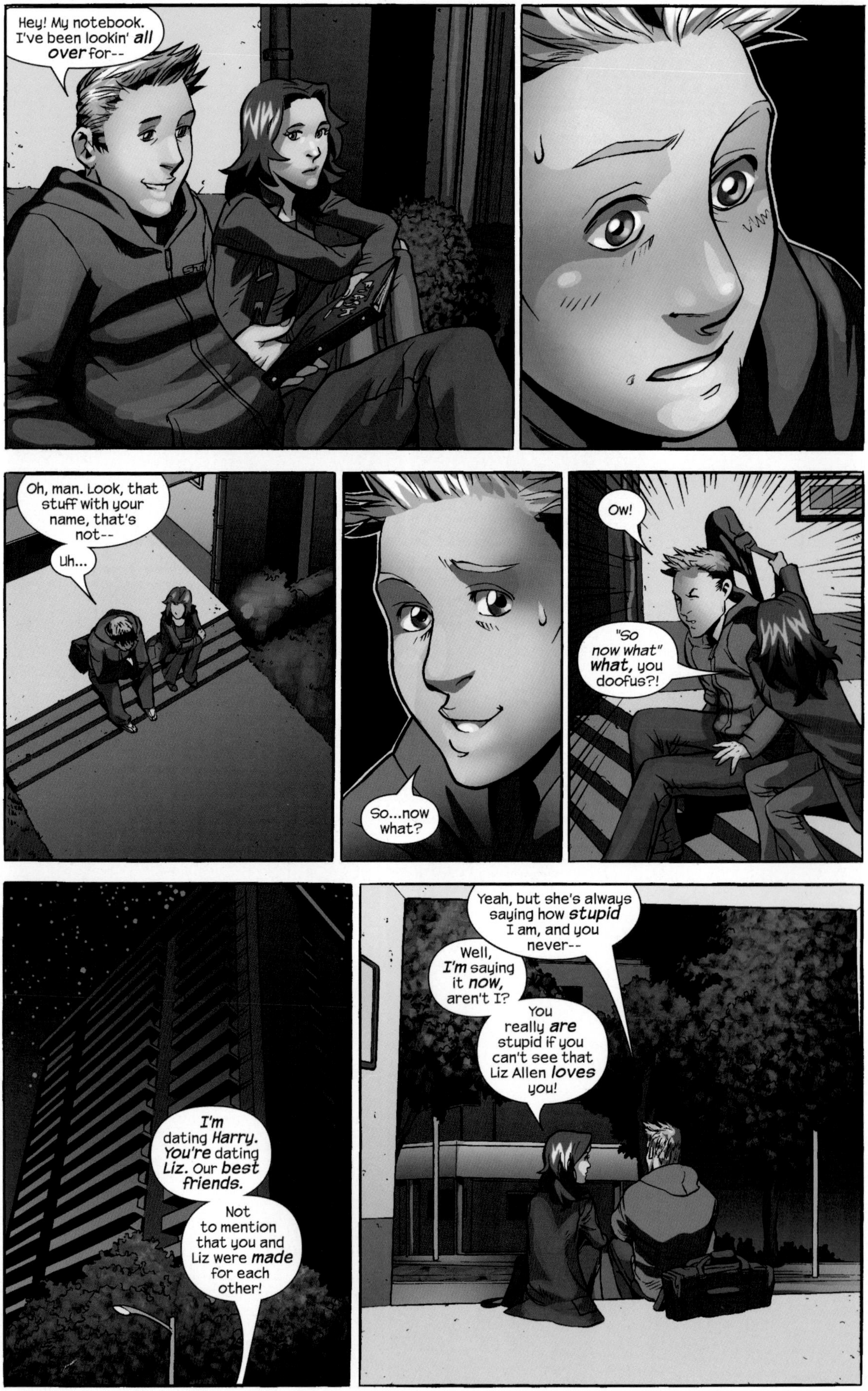
Hey! My notebook. I've been lookin' **all over** for--
Oh, man. Look, that stuff with your name, that's not--
Uh...
So...now what?
Ow!
"So now what" **what,** you doofus?!
I'm dating **Harry. You're** dating **Liz.** Our **best friends.**
Not to mention that you and Liz were **made** for each other!
Yeah, but she's always saying how **stupid** I am, and you never--
Well, **I'm** saying it **now,** aren't I?
You really **are** stupid if you can't see that Liz Allen **loves** you!

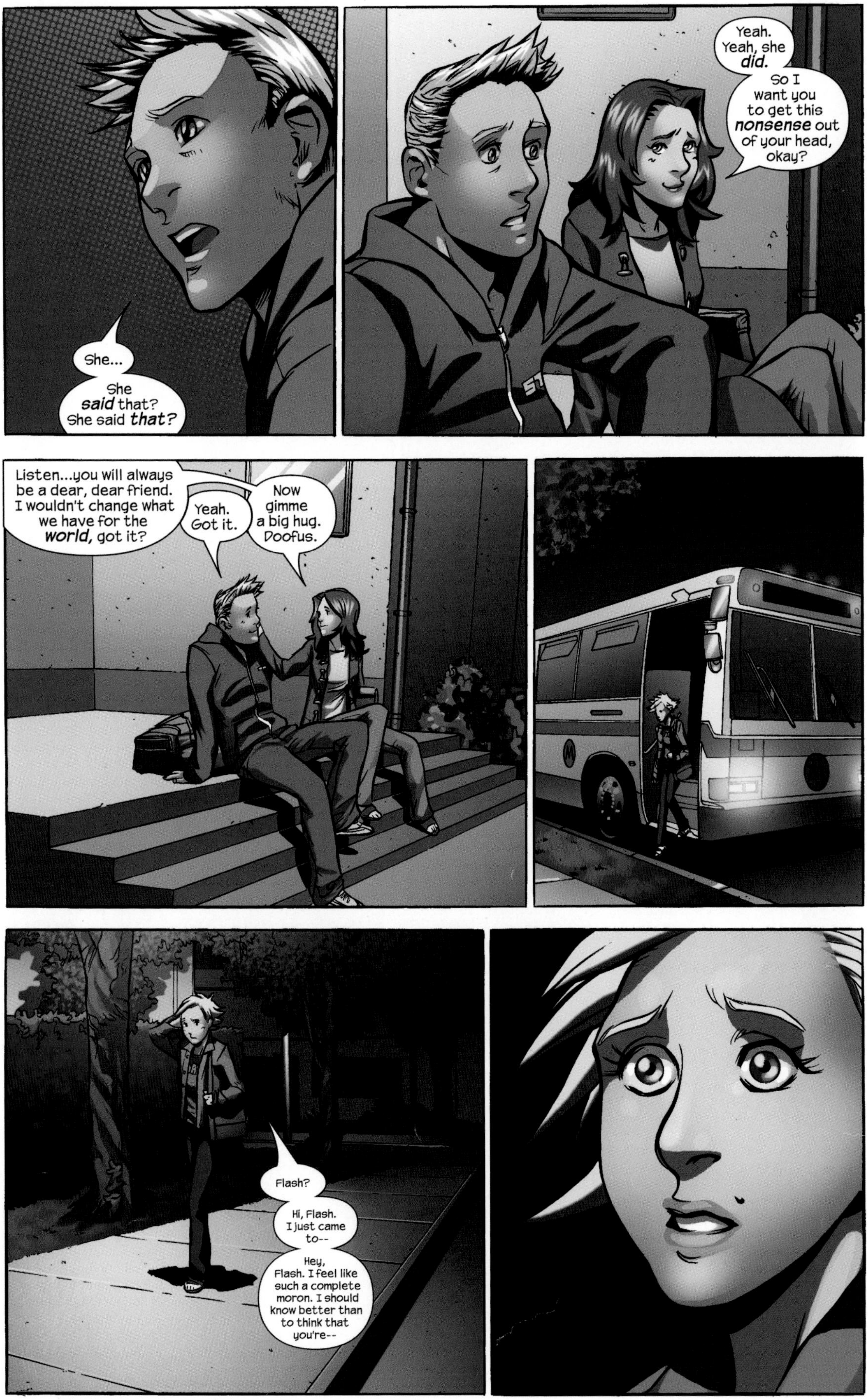
She...
She *said* that? She said *that?*
Yeah. Yeah, she *did.*
So I want you to get this *nonsense* out of your head, okay?
Listen...you will always be a dear, dear friend. I wouldn't change what we have for the *world,* got it?
Yeah. Got it.
Now gimme a big hug. Doofus.
Flash?
Hi, Flash. I just came to--
Hey, Flash. I feel like such a complete moron. I should know better than to think that you're--

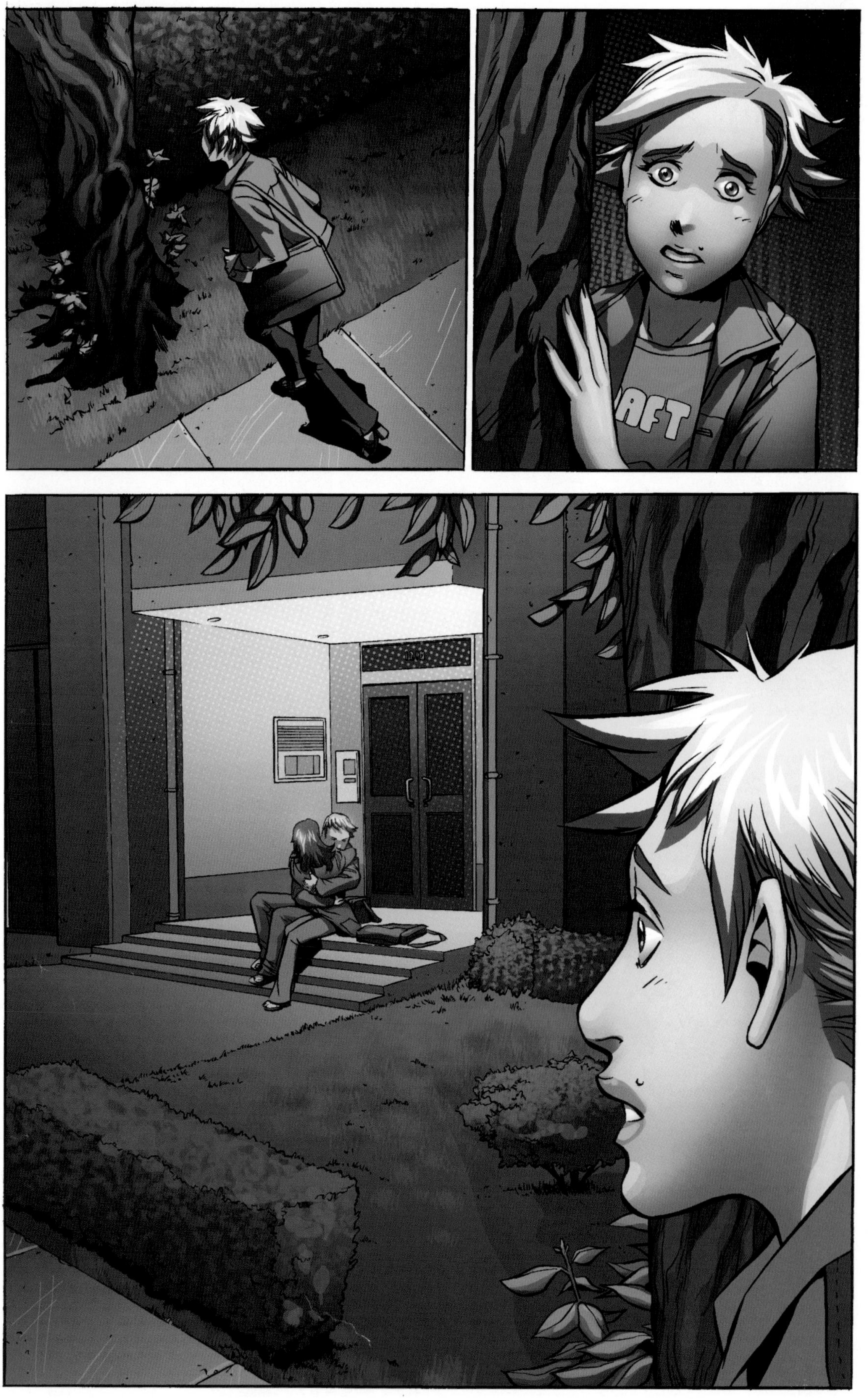